MW01242975

The Abbey Review Issue #2

Cover design by Hunter Bishop.
Edited by Hunter Bishop, Peter Schaub, & Katherine Curran.
Interior by Hunter Bishop.

Printed in the United States of America.

The Abbey Review

EST. 2021

Welcome to the Abbey Review

Hunter Bishop, Managing Editor

Whew. What a journey.

Getting this second issue out has been a lot more difficult than the first, but has been even more rewarding. To put out the first issue meant that we proved we could do it all, and so this second issue had to be even better. Pressure mounted, and personal lives (mostly mine) intervened

But here we are. Issue #2, of hopefully dozens and hundreds more. None of this would be possible without the brilliant authors who lend us their work so that we may happily, proudly, and with enormous gratitude show it off. This would not be possible without the hard work and patience of my co-editors, Peter Schaub and Katherine Curran, who have stayed the course no matter the waters.

This journal is real, and it's full of great work, and is built on hard work and determination and a little bit of desperation, too. I hope the person reading this, author or audience, enjoys these pieces as much as much as we have.

- Hunter

The Keeping

Philip Lisi

On the third floor,
The air is particled with old life—
When children drew
Broad-whiskered cats
And wrote leaden cursive
On lines of yellow tablet paper
The color of yarrow.

She keeps these things,
Carefully pressed together
In files labeled with our names,
Preserving what we might have been.

Sometimes I imagine
They whisper together,
These fragile parchments of the past,
Like papery wasps
Inside a dusty lamp shade:
"Do you remember
When they were young
And belonged to her?"

In winter, she ascends
To visit us in our youth,
Reminding herself of a time
When keeping and filing

Labored to fill a space
That would always be hollow.

After she is gone,
I must enter there,
And I find it hard to breathe.
Bound to sort through
What is left of us,
I am held between lives
Captured in time on fading pages
And want to burn them—
If only to martyr those memories
That once sustained
Something like love
And stifle the regret
That comes so quickly to me now.

What's in a Nickname?

Brianna Gaffney

A decade. Ten whole years. People have known each other for less time and gotten together. *What was I waiting for?*

The buzzer for baggage claim sounded and I came back to the present. I was struggling to get my mind right. One of my best friends was coming to pick me up from the airport soon. My friend of ten years. My *guy* friend of ten years. Throughout my entire trip, we texted and called every day.

"I should have come with you," he told me one night after I made it back to my Airbnb.

"No way," I laughed. The guy was a straight-A student on the Dean's list every semester. Med school was no joke and I didn't want to interfere with his dream in any way. I loved him too much for that. I had to get a hold of myself. *You can't tell him. Not now.*

"Bunny?" I'd know that nickname anywhere. I spun around fast, my elbow digging into something solid.

"Damn, Aria." He rubbed his stomach. My eyes zeroed in on his firm midsection.

Lord, give me strength.

"I'm sorry, Finn. You scared me." I went to touch him but pulled back. "Are you okay?"

He cooed, "I'm fine, see," he took my hand and placed it on his toned middle. I flinched and tugged my hand back, but he caught it. "You okay, Bunny?"

Shrugging, "I gotta grab my bag."

"Don't worry, I'll get it." He went to the rounder reaching for my large roller bag. His reach missed causing him to hustle through the other passengers to chase it down. Laughter burst out of me. This man was going to be the death of me. He returned with my luggage.

"Glad I could make you laugh." The Dennis Quaid smile formed on his face. Realization set in once again. I must tell him how I feel.

However, my bravery deserted me once we were in his car. We chatted about his study schedule for a big exam he had coming up. He did most of the talking while I

jumped in here and there. We arrived at his apartment complex where I left my car. He didn't exit right away, instead, shutting the car off and turning to me.

"You were kinda quiet. I thought you would be talking nonstop about your trip."

"Are you saying I talk too much?" It came off as if I was angry but I wasn't. Annoyed. I was annoyed at myself. Here I was on a seesaw. Anxiety was building up and I was ready to back out. "Where are my keys?"

"Upstairs." I exited the car and took the stairs. He hurried to follow. "Slow down." Walking into his living room, he turned to me. "What's wrong, Bunny?"

"Stop calling me Bunny." I felt bad getting irritated with him. He had been calling me that since we met sophomore year in undergrad. He was a witness to me always running around on my way somewhere, trying not to be late.

"I hate Alice in Wonderland," I muttered.
"What?"
"Nothing. It's getting late so—" A framed picture on the far wall stopped me from

continuing. I went to get a closer look. It wasn't just any picture, it was my first award-winning watercolor painting, A house on the marsh. He was so proud of me and loved the painting so much he begged (though there was no need) to keep it and frame it. "You still have it."

"Of course. Told you it was a masterpiece." His whispered words were in my ear. When did he get so close to me? I could feel the heat coming off his body.

"I need to tell you something." My courage had returned. I wanted to take a chance. Turning to him we came face to face. I never loved or wanted a person so much. He studied my face before closing his eyes and stepping back.

"It is getting late." His voice was now rough. I stood there confused. All of a sudden his mood changed. He placed my keys on the coffee table. I walked to grab them and he immediately crossed to the other side of the room.

"I know I should get going but," I sat on the edge of the table, "Listen, Finn, I've been thinking..." I looked at him and he had a face like thunder. Words left me. A heavy silence ensued. My heartbeat went into overdrive. *Run!*

"I'm sorry. I'm such a dingus. You need to study, don't you?" I rambled. His look softened but his body was stiff, hands stuffed in his pockets. I stood, defeated.

"Aria." Him using my real name was like a command. I started for the front door. "Stop," he moved quickly towards me and I retreated backward.

"Finn?" His mouth was suddenly on mine, my face enveloped in his large hands. The kiss bruising but passionate. We finally parted. "I should go," I whispered breathlessly. His lips found mine again. He kissed me deeper as if he was trying to devour me.

Pulling back, breathing hard, he spoke, "Do you really want to go?" I shook my head, my eyes focused on his chest. I couldn't look at him. *What was happening right now?* He took my chin in his hand and lifted my face so our eyes met. "Bunny, I need to hear you say it. Do you want to leave?"

"No. No, I don't." I took the initiative this time, rising on my toes. With a moan, he put his arms around me, lifting me. I immediately wrapped my legs around his waist. He backed us against the wall, pushing my dress up. His hands grasped my thighs holding me open for him. I let out a whine causing him to grind his erection against my center. Tugging my mouth away, "Oh my god."

Turning his attention to my neck, he left open mouth kisses up to my ear where he whispered huskily, "Are you wet for me, Bunny?" Laying another soft kiss on my neck I couldn't respond.

I gave a shaky nod.

Another grind but harder. "Use your words." He gave me a jostle, pushing me firmer into the wall. My underwear was yanked to one side as his fingers ran up my slit.

"Sh-h-it," I stuttered.

"Mm-hmm." He slipped a finger inside. "You're dripping." Then another one. The moan that escaped me was loud but smothered as he kissed my lips again. His fingers stroked my insides as his tongue tangled with mine. My underwear, still in his grasp, gave way, ripping.

"Finn..."
"Tell me," he pumped his fingers faster. "Please."
"Please what?"
I whimpered desperately.
"What did I say? Use your words."

"I want..." The craving was so strong but so was my embarrassment, which only made me more aroused. His fingers stilled.

"What do you want? Tell me and I'll give it to you."
"I want you. I-I need...you."
The sound of a zipper was my only warning. We locked eyes as he pushed inside

of me, taking my breath away.
"Bunny?" he caressed my cheek, "Aria, breathe, baby." I exhaled. He slowly

withdrew and thrust again. My mouth fell open, no sound coming out. He found his rhythm and set a pace. My climax hit me unexpectedly causing my nails to dig in his shoulders. "Fuck! You're so sensitive." He sped up the tempo. My bare backside continuously bumped against the wall.

"Yes. Yes, yes," I wept.

He pushed my legs wider, driving himself deeper. I gasped. A tingle began at my toes before traveling up to my gut like a streak of lighting. My hold on him tightened as my second climax took hold. I was pulled in tighter to his chest as he found his own. Cradled in his arms, I went limp and my head rested on his shoulder as a single tear escaped.

I awoke, hating myself for having yet another erotic dream about Finn. Having yet to confess my feelings had my subconscious on a rampage. I pushed my face into the pillow groaning. A strong arm encircled my waist and I froze. *Wait a minute.*

"You okay, Bunny?" He lay there shirtless, the sheets dangerously low on his hips. I quickly averted my eyes. "How are you feeling? I wasn't too rough with you, was I?"

I turned to him fully, my muscles protesting in the best way. "No. I...liked it." He gave me his memorable smile before pulling me into his arms.

Second Sight Rain

Olivia Stogner

That night the rain poured lightly
and dried my weeping
as I soaked through it
and gathered the waters
into my eyes.

I will not weep for you;
I will absorb your weeping—

empty armed mother
single twin
child who does not laugh
lone leaning grandfather

Take back—
yourself
that you may weep—
your fill.

The waters will not cover you;
I drink all you spill with my eyes.

Labyrinth

Rachel Elion Baird

I am dreaming of the lost
and the dying,
enter in the woodpeckers – bear birds,
tree eaters at the feeder,
long narrow beaks in the bath,
drinking gently of rain water
while joy birds circle like lions,
eat on stone and sand
before flying,
their hum just as sweet
as the chorus
sounding from the leaves of trees,
announcing, new land for the taking –
these electric ones,
beneath the shatter of breaking
abomination,
Mariupol, your dead babies
still inside their mothers' lifeless bodies
cracking time open to the sea,
a fissure forming there – turning;
Nightingale, the chosen,
landing to sing,
teach me by the rising sun
how all lines turn into spirals,
carry across on your wings.

TR_x

Greg Sapp

Dear Doctor Truth:

Who do you turn to, for advice? I suspect that when day after day you get dozens or maybe hundreds of letters and emails from people in every walk of life, everybody asking for your advice about what to do and how to do it, there has got to be times when you feel overwhelmed, plain and simple. So, I just wanted to thank you, because once I wrote looking for help, and I took your advice. Of course, it was right. It worked exactly the way you said that it would. Keep telling it like it is and doing what you do, and don't ever stop, please.

Sincerely, Your Number One Fan.

P.S. I know that you want to keep your identity secret, but lots of your followers want to know, at the very least: Are you a man or a woman?

Dear Number One Fan:

What I do is like an itch deep inside my head that I can only scratch by writing this column; but the more I do, the worse it gets. It's like a sick but adorable puppy that you take home and nurture back to health, only to have it grow into a slobbering, flea-bitten, ass-licking mongrel. If I could quit doing this, I would. To be honest, it's a burden and a frustration, and it does often feel like you readers don't deserve me. There's an important distinction that I think you're missing, though. I don't give anybody advice. I just tell them the truth. Many people aren't particularly thankful to hear it.

So, while I do appreciate your gratitude and encouragement, it won't change anything about what I do or how I feel about it. I have plenty of haters, too, and I cannot listen to them any more than I can let all of you sycophants who call yourselves "Truthers" go to my head. You're both pretty much the same to me. I've got a job to do.

And if being a fan meant that you have any respect for me, then you'd know by now that I can't reveal anything personal about myself – period, end of story. If people thought I was a dude, they'd question my advice about love or sex. If they thought I was a chick, they pay less attention to my opinions about money or politics. That's just true. So, I can't be any age or sex or race or religion, or have any loyalty other than to the ugly truth. Get real.

***

The visitor removed his headphones and got right to the point: "Yo, how do I get, wha's it called, financial aid?"

This was not the first time that financial aid had been the point of departure for a conversation with a potential student. Camille took a quick slam of her energy drink, then launched into her routine: "Thank you for your interest in Magnum College. We have an experienced staff that can explain all of your funding options. Have you chosen a program of study that you'd like to pursue?"

The young man shrugged, revealing a hangman's noose neck tattoo when he dropped his shoulders. "Not 'xactly. What d' yo suggest?"

It continually fascinated Camille how on a daily basis total strangers accosted her asking, essentially, what she thought they should do with their lives. These inquiries arrived mostly by email, text, or the college's Facebook or Twitter pages, and occasionally by phone, but still sometimes face-to-face, so when she did get drop-in business, she'd been trained to lead her clients into the executive conference room, in part because her office was always a mess, but also because, according to Dr. Estes Brown, the college president, it made people feel important, like they were going straight to the top.

"Let's discuss your goals," she said to the young man. "Follow me."

Among friends, Camille glibly referred to her position as "director of admissions," which was literally accurate, but also exaggerated because, in fact, she *was* the entire admissions department for Magnum College. She was the sole human being who responded to all queries sent to the anonymous "contact an advisor" link on the college's homepage. Most inquirers were motivated by the college's relentless marketing campaign, which included radio, television, newspapers, billboards, social media, and ubiquitous side-of-bus panels featuring Dr. Estes Brown himself, smiling with his arms-crossed, above a banner with school's motto: "Welcome to the Success Machine!" Camille understood very well that her task was to counsel – that is, to convince – these would-be students that one of the college's programs in office administration, retail management, criminal justice, laboratory technician, or substance abuse counseling was just the ticket to their future prosperity. It was easier than she'd imagined when she accepted the job, because most of the students were eager to believe Camille when she assured them that "By coming here today, you've taken a critical first step toward achieving your goals."

Camille invited the young man to sit at the head of the table and closed the door. "I'm Camille Jenkins," she said, giving his wrist an extra squeeze when shaking his hand. "What's yours?"

"My name is Heck. Heck Horton."

"Well, Heck, we have many excellent programs in challenging fields that are in high demand. Tell me a bit about yourself, so that I can help to place you..."

When Heck scratched his ear beneath the knit cap covering his head, Camille noticed a braided flame tattoo on his neck, over his shoulder blade and on the back of his hand (was it continuous, she wondered). She'd seen that same image spray painted under bridges and on the walls of vacant buildings around town, and she'd heard that it had some gang association.

"I got my GED," Heck began, sitting sideways in the chair.

"Excellent. That's a prerequisite for most of our programs. You're already well on your way." She noted how his lips were moving while she spoke to him, as if he was silently repeating everything she said. "What about your prior employment experiences?"

"I think, could be, I'd be interested in this criminal justice program. Is tha' like bein' a cop?"

"Our law enforcement certificate prepares students for an important career as a peace officer. Several of our graduates have gone on to serve in the Ohio State Patrol."

Camille pushed a program flyer toward him, and when he reached for it the "TR$_x$" chain around his neck slipped out from under the collar of his shirt. Camille saw it and felt a hot/ cold moral shiver skate down her spine. He was a Truther! Pushing away from the table, she looked both ways down the hallway outside of the conference room, then instead of returning to the seat across from Heck, sat next to him.

"Can I get real with you?" she asked.

"Truth is the only prescription," he replied using the catchphrase.

"Here's the deal, then. With those tattoos, you won't have a chance in hell of getting hired by any public police force. You just won't. And I'm not presuming anything, but I'm just telling it straight, so you should know that if you try to go into the private security business, they *will* do background checks. Do you understand what I mean?"

"Get real!" Heck hid a scowl behind a half-smile. "But tell me this much: Can I still get some of tha' financial aid?"

So that was his ploy. *'No judgment,'* Camille reminded herself – she was sometimes reluctant to embrace that aspect of Truthism. "Most likely," she answered.

"Then tha's what I want t' do."

Camille reached into a cabinet and found an admission form. "In that case, I'm endorsing you for our four quarter certificate program in criminal justice. Take this to Ms. Sofia Blanco, our financial assistance advocate, who can help you with your funding needs."

Heck looked at Camille and held his gaze. "What time d' yo' got off work?," he asked.

"No."

"What I asked ain't a yes 'r' no question. Let's be straight-up here: I'm asking yo' to meet me fo' a drink after work."

Camille began shaking from the inside out – anxiety, offense, anger… or just too much energy drink? "I understood perfectly what you said. And I said no."

Heck shook his head sideways. "Why fo' not?"

"Because I am not attracted to you. The only thing about you that I find even mildly appealing is that I know that my father would absolutely hate you. Mind you, I don't like those qualities in a person, either. I just like the effect that they have on my old man. Other than that, I have no interest in you. None."

"Tha's wack. But, hey, truth out," Heck said.

Camille did not return the acknowledgement, but at least, under the circumstances, she did not feel obliged to tell him "Welcome to the Magnum College family" at the conclusion of their interview. This encounter was just another episode in her life that reminded her that, despite its utility, decency, and conscience-liberating qualities, it was exactly like Doctor Truth said: "Sometimes telling the truth tastes just like eating shit."

***

Dear Doctor Truth:

I am a twenty three year old woman, living independently, with a secure job and an active, but selective and faith-based social life. When I was a teenager, I signed my church's virginity pledge. Then, when I met my fiancé, over a year ago, I was honest with him about my commitment to preserving my virginity until my wedding night, in order to honor my future husband and the sanctity of our marriage. He said that he shared my values, and that he was a virgin, too. I've accepted his marriage proposal, and we've been engaged for a month but haven't announced it yet. What bothers me, though, is that he says that, because we're now engaged, it is okay for us to

18

express ourselves sexually. Since we've already sworn our souls to each other for the rest of our lives, forsaking all others, he contends that we've already spiritually consummated our relationship, so there's no harm in doing it physically, too. He says that to do less is to hold back on making a complete commitment to our love. And I do love him. But a pledge is a pledge. What's the truth?

Yours, Chaste But Conflicted.

Dear Chaste But Conflicted:

*There is so much about your story that is just straight-up wrong at so many levels that I don't know where to start. I have absolutely no confidence in any kind of pledge, but especially if it a pledge **not** to do something. Self-denial never works in the long run, because it leads to confusion, doubt, regret. And it's much worse to regret something that you didn't do than one that you did. Furthermore, rather than rant about the flaws in any belief system that compels naïve vows from teenagers, or to point out the archaic, paternalistic attitude of treating virginity like a commodity, or even to cite sociological evidence that there is absolutely no correlation between "saving yourself" and eventual happiness in marriage… I could go on… Nevertheless,*

I will accept your statement as sincere and address just the question that you have posed.

My first advice is – run like hell.

Don't fool yourself. Your fiance' didn't suddenly change his mind or have some kind of new revelation on the subject of premarital sex. He's been playing you. Probably, he lacks confidence or doesn't have the balls to be straight with you (which may explain why he's still a virgin, if that's even true), but his obvious gambit has been to pay lip service to your values as a way to weasel into your panties, promising whatever it takes to make you believe what you're already predisposed to believe anyway, stringing you along until he figures that he has chipped away at your will to resist enough so that, finally, you will give in. This may have been his plan from the very start. Or, maybe he has some bogus way to rationalize it in his own mind. Either way, deep down, even if he has persuaded himself that he truly loves you, what matters to him most of all is getting between your legs. It cannot end well unless you cut him loose.

My second advice is – reconsider your pledge. Ask yourself: why did you make it in the first place, and what good is it doing you, anyway? You could do worse than to get yourself laid (safely), so in the future you won't have to worry about this stuff. Get real.

Doctor Truth

***

Truthers did not like to refer to their loose, informal association using any of the words that the media often employed, like "phenomenon," "movement," "cause," or the especially loathsome, "cult." To suggest that there was any organized structure to their nebulous confederation of like-minded but diverse and independent individuals merely divulged the ignorance of those who looked at them from the outside. When Truthers referred to themselves, they borrowed a phrase once used by Dr. Truth in the column, where s/he wrote:

Whatever folks are saying in the grapevine is true, whether it's factual or not.

Accordingly, they said that they belonged to a "grapevine."

Camille was proud that she had followed Dr. Truth from the very beginning, before it became a fad on social media. Three years earlier, when she first started working at Magnum College, she lunched every Friday at the Café Creekview, and while having her espresso and hummus bagel she'd peruse the new edition of the weekly Columbus Buzz, the alternative community news rag. At that time, the paper featured a marginally popular syndicated column by Anastasia the Advice Guru. Camille always read it because it was mindless fluff and satisfied her harmless voyeuristic curiosity – certainly not because she ever found it to be helpful or even particularly insightful. One week, the Buzz published a letter to the editor that was harshly critical of the Advice Guru's previous column, in which Anastasia had recommended that "Can't Compete" demand that her husband get professional counseling for his admitted "pornography addiction." The author of this rebuttal, though, contended that there is no such thing as a pornography addiction, and that:

> Can't Compete's husband only said that he was "addicted" because he knew that he'd gotten busted dead-to-rights and didn't have the guts to stand up for himself, so he pleaded that he was addicted to play for some sympathy.

Then, the letter writer flipped the accusation, asserting that, far from being symptomatic of a dependency, looking at pornography is common and entirely normal:

> Because absolutely nobody's first reaction upon seeing a picture of two adult people having sex is to look away. Pretending to be shocked is just hiding guilty titillation.

The letter went on:

If his only use for pornography is, presumably, jerking off, what's the problem? I think that the answer is in how she signed the letter. If "Can't Compete" feels inadequate, that's on her, because almost by definition, nobody can compete with fantasies. Fortunately, nobody has to. People only compete with reality. Fantasies are no harm, no foul.

And furthermore:

Ultimatums are for judges. And prescribing therapy is for professionals. For a dime-store advice columnist to order treatment for a non-existent mental health disease is nothing less the criminal malpractice.

The letter was signed: *Get Real. Doctor Truth*

Soon thereafter, the Buzz dropped Anastasia the Advice Guru's column, and in its place, a new feature, "Get Real with Doctor Truth" appeared.

It was a year or more before Camille began noticing the red and gold "Get Real" bumper stickers showing up on mostly late model cars around The Ohio State University campus and on lamp posts in working class neighborhoods across the metropolitan area. The slogan became popular on t-shirts, for not only did it identify the person as a "Truther" (a term popularized by the grapevine), but it

23

conveyed the tacit message to anybody who understood the code that that they were obliged to drop all pretext (that is, "speak truth") if they wished to engage the wearer in any kind of social interaction. Various other forms of paraphernalia were sold on Web sites and mailed from a post office box in Pataskala. There was a line of jewelry based upon the TR$_x$ (i.e., Prescription, Truth) motif. (Camille wore an ankle bracelet at work and two black diamond earrings when she went clubbing.) Other forms of swag consisted of coffee cups, baseball caps, refrigerator magnets, belt buckles, and posters bearing quotes from Doctor Truth. Somewhat more seditious, to some people's minds anyway, was that around town – spray painted on walls and street signs on North High Street, on the sides of vacant buildings in Linden and Clintonville, and, for some reason, on manhole covers in Gahanna and Reynoldsburg – a stenciled, silhouetted image representing Dr. Truth began to appear. It was a hooded figure, neither male nor female, with eyes concealed over round cheeks and a dimpled chin framing a crooked, half-smirking grin – sort of a cross between Little Bo Peep and the Unabomber. To Truthers, it meant that the Doctor was watching them.

Who was Doctor Truth, really? Folks tended to believe that the Doctor resided in the greater Columbus environs, because, despite its popularity the column remained exclusive to the Buzz. (Some disciples began referring to Columbus as "Truth City," where rural and urban collide, Appalachia flattens out, the Rust Belt collapses, and the Midwest begins – where else could the plain truth be better grasped?) In general, men seemed to think that she was a woman, and women believed that he was a man. And there were transgendered theories, too. (Personally, Camille envisioned Doctor Truth's words coming out with masculine volume, emphasis and effect… but also, critically, with feminine sincerity and conviction; so she could go either way.) One central tenet of Truthism was that the Doctor could be anybody, anywhere. It kept them honest, some liked to say.

In the weekly columns, Doctor Truth wrote nothing to acknowledge, much less encourage the enterprise of these followers. But when the Doctor launched a Twitter account, it seemed like implied validation of the burgeoning cottage industry. Through this medium, the grapevine's popularity spread, via a single, memetic remark that Doctor Truth posted every day, and which went viral through subsequent sharing, re-tweeting, and commentary. Things like:

- Nobody ever won an argument just by being right.
- Disappointment is the fulfillment of unrealistic expectations.
- Time heals all wounds, except fatal ones.
- Trust a liar to keep your secrets more than an honest person.

- Teamwork most benefits the least productive member of any team.

- Whether the glass is half full or half empty depends on if you are filling it or drinking from it.

- One hundred percent of all things are more complicated than ninety-nine percent of the people think.

- Luck only works for people who don't need it.

- A habit is like an ugly baby – you only love it if it's yours.

- Be brief – because nobody's paying attention anyway.

Every day the Doctor tweeted to the legions of Truthers another equally quirky, profound, paradoxical, ironic or ambiguous nugget of wisdom to contemplate. Blogs were launched for the sole purpose of deconstructing the Doctor's words. Meetings were held in coffee shops and vape lounges and arts studios. (Camille had gone to a regular meeting in the Short North for a while, but it felt eerily similar to her father's call-and-response rituals of Alcoholics' Anonymous, which seemed utterly un-Truth-like to her, so she quit.) Furthermore, codes of conduct evolved. By tacit agreement, Truthers did not shake hands or bump fists when they met; they extended their open palms in front of themselves. Instead of hello or goodbye, they said "Get Real." Above all, the most unifying and defining feature of Truther-to-Truther interactions was that the members understood implicitly that they were never, under any circumstances, to lie, fib, feign, exaggerate, deceive, dissimulate, pretend, prevaricate, or otherwise bear false witness with or to one another.

That, Camille had discovered, was harder said than done. Telling the truth was of limited usefulness, since it didn't necessarily make her a better, more popular, or a more successful person. It did, however, give her a flash of exhilaration, which she liked, a lot. Telling the truth was a cheap thrill, so long as she could get away with it.

***

Driving to work, Camille sipped her coffee while passing the giant billboard on Taylor Station Road, where an aggressively beaming likeness of Doctor Estes Brown stood in an open-armed, greeting pose against a yellow background, next to the caption in bold letters that cast shadows: "Welcome to Magnum College." Passing it felt like being watched. The campus of Magnum College was in a suburban office and industrial complex on a re-developed brownfield, now planted with dogwood trees and traversed by paved bike paths, which was close enough to the airport so that, even in her windowless office, Camille could hear jets landing all day long.

There was just one building, with offices on the first floor, classrooms on the second floor, and a "student center" with vending machines, video games, a pool table, and a television that was never turned off. The last thing that Camille did every day before entering through the revolving doors was pin her name tag above her heart.

Sofia Blanco was re-filling a kiosk in the lobby with flyers. "*Buenos dias*," she chirped.

Not really, Camille thought. "Good morning to you," she said.

"Watch out." Sofia covered one side of her face with the flyers and whispered conspiratorially. "Doctor Brown, he is in a *loco* mood today."

Camille shrugged. She actually preferred Doctor Brown's occasional griping and minor peevishness to his default public personality, which was overbearingly optimistic, affirmative, and gregarious. He used both hands when shaking hands, and turned it into a hug if there was sustained eye contact. (He'd once hugged the local chief of police, who had no choice but to hug him back.) At meetings with the board of trustees, he sometimes broke into song – *I can see clearly now, the rain has stopped. I can see all obstacles in my way...* (He claimed that he'd once been a Pip, but Sofia researched it and confirmed that he was just kidding.) When working his charm upon a room of people, especially one populated with potential donors, Estes Brown was like a sculptor shaping human clay. Even people who couldn't stand him, loved him.

Camille entered her office, where the wallpaper on her computer screen was the Magnum College seal, a crown set in a triangle, with the words MAGNUM and COLLEGE along the ascending legs, and beneath the base, in a banner, *Fac et Spera – MMV.* The name tag that she wore also bore this symbol. Within a month after starting her job at Magnum College, Camille had taken down the framed diploma of her master degree in communication from Ohio State University, and put in its place a certificate of completion of Magnum College's continuing education program in office administration. Potential students whom she was interviewing often asked her if Magnum College was "hard," to which she replied, "If I can do it, anybody can."

An hour into responding to her daily email queries ("We're honored that you are considering entrusting your future to Magnum College"), Estes Brown summoned Camille into his office. "How goes it, Ms. Jenkins?" he called to her.

"Good morning, sir."

Dr. Brown was sitting, not behind his desk (where, the joke was, he only sat to have his picture taken), but in an upholstered wingback chair in front of a coffee table in the corner of his office.

He gestured for her to sit and offered to get her a cup of coffee. "Thanks," she said, taking a gulp and hoping for a caffeine surge.

Dr. Brown spoke before she could take another sip. "I've been looking at the third quarter enrollments report..."

"Our numbers are up."

"Yes. Congratulations. But..." he waved his fingers criss-cross. "There are certain demographics where I see room for improvement."

What's he talking about?, she wondered – *Black, Hispanic, worker retraining, and women in every category are all higher than last year. Even disabled students have increased. Few Asians, but they seemed to want to have nothing to do with Magnum College.*

"Such as?," she asked.

"Veterans. Our national heroes, back home from Iraq and Saudi Arabia." (*Saudi Arabia?*, Camille wondered. Dr. Brown was wearing an American flag lapel pin – had he put that on just for this talk?) "I believe that we need to recruit more of them. And, there are several financial support programs, just for them. We need to be more entrepreneurial."

So, that's what this is about, Camille thought, *Getting a piece of federal aid money.*

"I agree," she said. "What can we do to be of greater assistance to them?"

Dr. Brown popped crossed his legs and rubbed his hands together. "You need to do some marketing…" And Camille listened as he expounded upon what specific tasks he expected her to undertake in service to this objective, the whole time thinking *blah, blah, blah,* even while repeatedly nodding up and down.

Upon being dismissed, Camille had not taken twenty steps after leaving Dr. Brown's office before Sofia approached from behind, her hoop bracelets jingling when she landed her hand on Camille's shoulder. "Wait up, girlfriend. *¿Que paso?"*

Of all the women who worked at Magnum College, Camille had observed that she was the only one whom Sofia ever addressed as "girlfriend." It was curious, given that Camille had always been wary of Sofia's reputation as a gossip; still, it felt kind of ingratiating to be thought of in that way. She was weighing her response when, under the pressure of Sofia's stare, she said: "Nothing."

"Oh, *¡no manches!*. Come on, girlfriend, I know that the doctor is scheming something – tell me."

"He wanted to speak with me about enrollments."

"I knew so. What about these enrollments? Give me a hint. This is my deal, too."

There, she had a point. The notion blinked through Camille's mind that she wished Sofia was a Truther, so she could speak to her with candor and honesty, and not freak her out.

"Do you want to go to lunch?"

"Do I? Yes! Now? Let's us do!"

Sofia opened her purse to rummage for change for the vending machines, when Camille intervened by suggesting that they go "off campus;" she would drive. Sofia wiped her feet before getting into Camille's Prius. Camille suggested that they grab a bite at the Olde Towne Plaza.

"We're going to the plaza? For really?"

Sofia confessed that she'd always wanted to go there, as if it was Champs Elysees and not downtown Gahanna, Ohio. Still, her enthusiasm was infectious, which gave Camille the satisfying sense that she was expanding Sofia's horizons. On their way into the Café Creekview, Camille picked up the latest edition of the Columbus Buzz from the stack by the front counter. A server took them to a seat on the patio, under an umbrella, surrounded by herbs and flowers. Sofia waited for Camille to order, and then asked for the same thing.

Among Truthers, there was frequent discussion and several opinions concerning if, when, whether, and how it was appropriate to introduce a novice to Doctor Truth's grapevine. (Some called it "conversion.") Camille had never attempted this with anybody, and with Sofia it was hard to get in a word edgewise, but after the meal, while waiting for the check, she casually opened the Buzz and asked, "Have you ever read this Doctor Truth column before?"

"No. Should I, do you think?"

"Well…" Camille told herself to tread lightly. "I'm sure that you've seen those bumper *Get Real* bumper stickers around town."

"Ay! I've seen them, oh sure. Is that about these things? What is it all for?"

"I'm kind of a fan." Camille folded the newspaper. "Take this. Read it."

"I will do it."

When the check came, Camille snatched it and insisted on paying. Sofia gushed "*gracia*s," her eyes wide and damp. They were late returning to the office, sneaking in a side door, thus sealing their bond with minor criminality.

***

Dear Doctor Truth:

For four months, I have been dating a well-educated, professional man, who, at 45 years of age, is considerably older than me. The relationship has been emotionally and physically satisfying, but there is still something about him that feels "off," out of synch, insincere. When he brought up the subject of moving in together, I hesitated, explaining that while I love him, I wasn't sure if I was ready. That wasn't entirely true, though. Because of my doubts, I ordered a background check on him from an online investigative service. It turns out that twice in the last ten years he has been arrested for drunk driving. Now, I cannot help but wonder what else he might be hiding. Should I confront him with what I know? Or, should I wait and see if he comes clean?

Gratefully, Past Behavior is the Best Indicator of Future Performance.

Dear Past Behavior:

This relationship is doomed. But I put that mostly on you. In any adult relationship people have to make decisions about whether and how to address issues about their past, of which they might not be proud (and that he is older than you is obviously pertinent, since that means he's carrying more baggage). In many cases, I think that the best answer is – never.

Everybody is a product of consequences. Some are obvious or inescapable. Fortunately, most of the

34

stupid things that people do have consequences that come with a statute of limitations. Beyond that, nothing is a consequence unless you choose to make it one.

There's a common myth that a successful relationship depends upon being entirely forthright about every sin, every flaw, and every mistake you've ever made. Some people say that's the basis of trust, without which you can't have a relationship. Nonsense! You can love a person completely, and still keep secrets from him. Relationships aren't about trust. They are about acceptance. But I don't think that you're willing to take that chance.

Background checks can't test for heart, for intent, for attitude -- only for mistakes. If that's what really matters to you, get used to being lonely. Get Real.

Doctor Truth.

***

Camille was driving so fast that she almost missed it, but as she was approaching the billboard at the entrance to Magnum

College, something unexpected pricked her peripheral vision; she slammed the brakes and looked up. Next to the brilliant visage of Doctor Estes Brown, somebody had spray painted in large, loopy letters,

TR$_x$

Seeing this, Camille honked the car's horn; it just felt like the right thing to do.

At work, Camille gulped energy drinks while composing her strategic report for marketing Magnum College to veterans. Among her recommendations was creating a new position for a "veterans services advisor," which she knew that Dr. Brown would ask her to do, in addition to her current responsibilities; but she'd also decided that when he did, she'd use it as leverage for requesting a raise. She wanted a travel budget, too -- maybe the doctor would send her to the annual conference in Orlando. To demonstrate that she was being "entrepreneurial," she included in the report a lengthy list of grants, scholarships, aid programs, and foundation funds available to veterans, with a page header of clip art images of dollar signs. She put her name prominently on the byline, even though she figured that by the time it was presented to the board of trustees, Estes Brown would have replaced hers with his. That was okay, if it profited her.

Nobody ever got anywhere without being taken advantage of. Getting used to that ineluctable fact was part of getting real.

Around 11:30 am, Camille pushed back from her desk and went to the rest room. Sitting on a bench in the hall, Heck Horton was bent over his cell phone, playing Candy Crush. Camille paused, and then accelerated, attempting to walk by him without being noticed, but when Heck finished a level in the game, he looked up and their eyes snapped into place.

"Yo, yo, yo, 'sup Ms. Advisor?"

Camille stopped. "Aren't you supposed to be in class?"

"Be easy. Ain't nothing in class 'xcept a video talkin' head on a big screen, wha' don't take no attendance or give no quizzes, so I decided tha' I ain't got need t' be there."

"You are paying for the privilege of taking those classes."

"I'm takin' the money, but it ain't me what's paying tuition."

Camille felt a pinch of indignation in her temples.

Heck gestured with open palms. "Hey, truth is truth. Am I right? No judgment, remember?"

"Okay, but look… Hanging around here when your class is meeting doesn't look good. At least be discreet."

"I ain't hangin'. I'm waitin' fo' somebody." Heck stood, allowing his pants to droop well below the waistline of his boxers. "And there she comes."

Sofia approached from down the hall. Camille pivoted in the opposite direction and continued into the women's room, where she slipped into the first empty stall and sat with her head in hands, fending off an incipient migraine. She remained there for twenty minutes.

That afternoon, Camille left her office door open just a crack and lowered the blinds in the window. Her feet itched, so she took off her shoes, then her socks, but the more that she scratched, the farther up her legs the sensation spread. At one point, while she was re-re-reading her report, she felt a sudden stinging sensation high on her left calf, and reaching to dig in with her fingernails, she knocked a nearly full can of energy drink onto her desk. The bubbly, piss-colored liquid cascaded over the papers. Camille started sopping up the mess, using one sheet of tissue at a time, before she grunted with disgust and swept everything into the wastebasket.

On the other side of the door, pressing her face so that just one of her eyes and a corner of her mouth could be seen in its narrow opening, Sofia hazarded to ask, "Are you in there okay, girlfriend?"

"This is bullshit!," Camille exclaimed, surprising herself.

"¡Qué va!" Sofia let herself in, closing the door behind her. "Tell me what is the problem."

Camille realized that she must look ridiculous, with one pants leg pulled up to her knee and a wet spot on her crotch. Instinctively, she sought to deflect the subject away from herself. "Did you go to lunch with that Mister Horton?"

Pressing her palm against her chest, Sofia said: "I was going to talk to you about him – really, I was."

"It's not my business, but…"

"Not so. I want your opinion. He has been making talk with me. I think he is a bit some cute – *si?* For tonight, he has asked me to go out with him. I said okay, but I think that you saw him first, so if I've gotten into your way…"

Camille gestured palms-up to Sofia, then pointed for her to sit and waited until they were at eye level before articulating, with staccato emphasis: "This is the truth: I am ab-so-lute-ly *not* attracted to Heck Horton in any way what-so-ever."

More puzzled than relieved, Sofia asked: "Why not?"

If Heck Horton had walked into the room at that very moment, Camille would have said the same thing: "Take my advice, girlfriend. Don't believe a single word that comes out of his mouth."

***

Sofia did not follow Camille's advice. Camille surmised that she felt guilty about it, so she was sly about seeing Heck; she left work and went to the bus stop, like always, but waited for him to pick him up there. Within the college building, the two of them exchanged and an *hola* and a "yo, yo, yo" when they passed, but they did not linger in each other's company. Still, to Camille, their relationship was obvious; she could see it, first, in the shit-eating smirk on Heck's face when he walked by Camille, as if he was gloating "I got her and there ain't nothin' yo' can do 'bout it," and, second, more poignantly, in how Sofia had ceased referring to her as "girlfriend."

Camille reasoned that she really shouldn't care. She was too busy to concern herself with Sofia's ill-considered love life. For a month, she'd been making calls and visits to every veterans' service agency in ten counties promoting the "You've Served Your Country. Now, Let Magnum College Serve You" campaign (the motto was her idea). That week, while he was attending the national Veterans' Career Assistance Network Conference in Orlando, Doctor Estes Brown had left Camille in charge of the college ("Don't burn the house down," he'd said to her). It was a consolation prize, although with significant symbolic significance.

40

"Should I salute?," Heck Horton asked Camille while passing in the hall.

"Bite me," she replied.

On the Friday before Doctor Brown was scheduled to return, Camille was getting ready to leave for a long lunch when her phone rang. It was Sofia. "Can I come to speak with you, Camille?," she asked.

That she was asking for permission felt awkward. "Now is not a good time."

"*Por favor,* I am already here…" Sofia was on the cell phone just outside of Camille's office. She pushed the door open wider, so that Camille could see that Heck Horton was standing beside her. .

Go away, Camille thought; "Not here," she blurted. Sitting, she felt defensive, so in order to generate some indignation, she stormed between Sofia and Heck, leading them to the conference room. Sofia followed swiftly, but Heck dragged his feet. Once inside the room, they all remained standing.

"Whatever you want to tell me is none of my concern," Camille asserted.

"I think not so…," Sofia started. Pulling back her hair, she uncovered a silver TR_x pin on her collar. "Can we *get real?*"

Although she'd suspected the worst between Sofia and Heck, this, somehow, seemed worse than the worst. "When did you...?"

Heck jumped in: "Yo' answer is s'posed to be: Truth is the only prescription."

"I know the password, thank you very much. You want the truth? I think that you're making a mistake, Sofia. And, you, Mr. Horton, are using her... *to get back at me."*

"¿Por qué?

"Say what?"

Camille hadn't intended to say that last part out loud. "Truth is truth," she insisted. *Or, was it?*

"That is not so," Sofia objected. "Speak truth – is this what you believe?"

"Or is tha' just what yo' is sayin' 'cause, deep down, yo' is jealous?"

"No, no, no... *you* get real! Sofia, you want me to give you my blessing even though I disapprove. And you, Mr. Horton, are just playing another scam, because that's how you roll."

The three stood looking at each other, sideways one way then sideways the other, a Mexican standoff in which each of them aimed Truth at the others like a lethal weapon. Camille wasn't sure if the angst in her gut was rage, disgust, or trepidation. Exasperated, or looking for an escape, or both, she bent over, wrapped the chain of her ankle TR$_x$ bracelet around her thumb, and snapped it off suddenly, tossing it at Heck Horton.

"I quit!," she proclaimed. Immediately, she felt lighter. "I wish both of you happiness," she lied.

***

Dear Doctor Truth:

How do you know that the people who write to you aren't completely making up their problems and situations? For that matter, how do we know that you aren't from some corporate marketing department, and that the character of Doctor Truth isn't just a fabricated brand, and that in reality there is no such person as you?

Suspiciously, An Informed Consumer

Dear Informed Consumer:

Finally, somebody gets it! My job here is done. Stay real.

Doctor Truth

Anchored

Noah Kenney

It was early in the morning. It was grey and rainy outside, and the sun had no power as it rose through waterlogged clouds. The wind came through the bedroom window and Martin could feel it in his chest. He stepped out of bed and dressed into sweatpants and a thermal shirt. The dog jumped around the room, making the floor tremble and the pennies on the nightstand rattle.

"Relax. Relax, boy," Martin said.

Martin dug up his thick wool socks from the hamper. Critter put his nose in the hamper and tossed the dirty clothing. Martin whistled and Critter snapped to attention, thumping his big ass on the carpet. Martin sat on the edge of the bed and put his socks on. He looked at the lump of blankets in bed. He sat there for a moment and thought something bitter about his wife. Then he walked out of the room, letting Critter pass before closing the door. Sometimes Martin gave Betsy a kiss before he walked the dog. But he stopped doing that so much. Betsy usually buried her head under the covers and pretended to sleep, anyway.

"Come on. Come on, boy," Martin said as he shook the leash.

The driveway was darkened with rain, and Martin was trying to coax the dog into the backyard. Critter wouldn't go on wet grass. Martin had to walk him around the block a few times until he couldn't hold it anymore. Sometimes he was so stubborn that he'd take a shit on the side of the road. Critter was too big to pull onto the grass. And Martin knew that Betsy didn't walk Critter as much as she said, so he'd feel guilty if he didn't get the dog exercise in the morning.

Martin often came home to a house that smelled like shit.

"You have to walk him," he'd say to his wife. "It smells like shit. The house is gonna permanently smell like shit."

Martin fed the dog. He had to get this expensive dog food because Critter had crystals in his urine a few months ago. Something with his kidneys. The dog was getting older. The dog was initially a present for Max. Max was just eight at the time, and he didn't get along with the other boys in the neighborhood. Martin wanted to get Max a friend that would grow with him. They'd look after each other. A boy and his dog.

What else is there to say? Max went to college across the country. He got a small scholarship from Penn State, but he chose to go to Portland. Martin didn't push him either way. It's understandable for a young man to want some distance from his home. It's just one of those things. Distance can be good. Martin leaves his son's bedroom door open so Critter can nap in there. Betsy hadn't left the house since her mother died. Old age. It was bound to happen. Betsy lost her job at the pharmacy. That put them in a tough spot. They had the dog, the house, Max's college. It's the fortunate things you acquire when you live a straight life, but it's a lot for a man. It's more than it seems.

Betsy's mother was in her eighties, so it wasn't a tragedy the way Martin saw it. He'd been asking her to see a therapist. They'd find the money for it. She'd get upset and say that she's an orphan. He needs to show compassion. He'd say, "Bets, you're fifty years old." He'd say, "Bets, you know I love you." There were times when she admitted that her level of grief was probably something deeper and more complex, and maybe therapy would help. She never called the doctor. She never tried making sense of it.

Martin showered and dressed himself for work. He recently stopped shaving, and in the shower he liked to fold his lower lip against the wet hair on his chin. His father had a beard. He died when Martin was in his twenties. Liquor. The liver. He and Betsy married a few weeks after the funeral. Martin got a promotion at the hardware store, and soon after they got pregnant with Max. Life moved fast. Now everything felt slow. Time was anchored by all this... all this.

The hardware store was down the street. It was past a long stretch of road with a corn field on one side and a thick of trees on the other. Rain drizzled onto the windshield, and Martin let it scatter and blur his vision. Finally he hit the wipers. It was the beginning of March. Birds had come back to Pennsylvania for spring. Black birds with orange bellies hopped along the side of the road and flew around close to the earth.

Either side of the road, the trees or the corn field, would be a fine way to disappear.

TWO BOYS FISHIN', CUSSIN', AND TALKIN' ABOUT SEX

Sandy Moffett

Salamander Creek is six feet across at its widest, hardly more than a trickle, rocky, with a few, very few, pools that might be three or four feet deep. The water is as clear as an autumn sky. A couple of suckers and some horny-head chubs are visible, finning slowly to stay in place, making quick darts up current to snatch something edible, flashing like new quarters as the current carries them back to their stations. The stream meanders down a shallow valley full of beeches and birches and rhododendron, before it disappears in the roiling tumble of the Elk River. Arlo Gilliam and Johnny Banner, both 11, in faded overalls and short sleeved shirts, sit on the bank with willow poles, the heaviest thread they could find in their mothers' sewing baskets tied on, and bent-pin hooks, drifting worms through the deepest hole. Arlo, with curly brown hair, is almost a foot taller than blonde Johnny, but their weight is pretty much the same.

The smell of the found cigarette butt they shared lingers. Arlo explores behind his right ear with his index finger. Turns his head toward Johnny.

"What's that?"

"What's what?"

"Behind my ear—bump."

"Can't see nothin' but hair."

Arlo moves his hair out of the way, "Where my finger is—see?"

"Um, no—yeah. Whoa—that's a tick. Big tick."

"Agkh, get it off—pull it off."

"Looks like a raisin."

"Don't care what it looks like—get the damn thing off."

"You don't have to cuss."

"Just pull the goddamn thing off."

"Can't just pull it off. You'll get spotted rock fever. I read about that in *Field and Stream*. Gotta put some'm hot on it."

"Just get it off."

Johnny reaches in all his pockets and finally pulls out a book of matches, opens it. There are two left. He lights one, blows it out, and aims the still-red end toward the tick. The smell of scorched hair replaces that of tobacco.

Arlo jerks away. "Oowww, shit!"

"Sorry. My hands are shakin' an' yer wigglin'. Ya gotta hold still. I missed it."

Johnny lights another match and blows it out. He aims the glowing stem at Arlo's neck.

"Oowww. Fuck." Arlo reaches behind his ear and pulls the tick off, throws it on a rock and steps on it. Blood squirts on his shoe.

"Jesus Christ, Johnny."

"You don't need to cuss, Arlo. You're gonna go straight to hell."

"Who says?"

"My Ma. Says it's in th' Bible. Two things that'll send you to hell quicker'n anything. Cussin', 'specially with His name, 'n. . ." Johnny pauses.

"Yeah, 'n what's two?"

"That other thing."

'What other thing?"

"Ya know."

"Don't know—what other thing?"

Johnny makes a loose fist with his right hand and pumps it up and down toward his crotch. He is starting to giggle—struggling to hold it back. "Ya know."

Arlo starts to giggle. He tries to say something, then gives up.

Now Johnny is laughing. He can't stop.

Finally, Arlo, "No I don't know. What other…" He can't finish through his own laughter.

Johnny, "Whack. . . (hoot) Whack. . .(wa ha ha) Whackin'." He can't finish.

Arlo, trying to catch his breath, mimicking Jonny's pantomime. "I don't care if I do die, do die, do die."

They can hardly sit up now, they're laughing so hard. Finally, they slow down. They breathe deeply. They look into the pool for a long time, each with his own thoughts.

Then Arlo, wiping tears from his eyes. "What if somebody does it for you?"

"What? Does what for you?"

"Ya' know. What you said."

"What'r you talkin' about?"

"Ya' know, somebody."

"Somebody? Who, somebody?"

"Oh, I du'no. . .Rosalee maybe."

"Shut up."

"What about Rosalee?"

"Shut up."

"Ros-a-lee."

"Goddammit, shut up."

They look at each other. Johnny turns away.

Pause.

Arlo breaks the silence.? "What about shit? Wha's your Ma say 'bout shit?"

"Shit ain't in th' Bible."

Johnny drifts his worm through the current half-heartedly. He turns to Arlo. "What's goin' on, you 'n Jack Lowe?"

"Nothin'"

"I know you wuz in a fight."

"OK. So you know

"You wuz in the principle's office. Got a whuppin' didn't ya?"

Loudly. "Nothin' I said."

Johnny waits for Arlo to go on. He doesn't. Finally he checks his hook. "Fish ain't gonna bite no more—anyhow I gotta git home."

"Me too. Mama's gonna yell at me. Guess I'm late already." Arlo looks into the water. "Wisht we coulda caught one of them big suckers. Ma's gotta couple tater sacks in the spring house. I might could sneak one out 'n we can make a seine. Catch one of them big suckers. Wish we coulda' fished in Elk River. Mighta' caught us one of them trouts. Don't know why they got them posted signs—ain't nobody ever fishes down there. Them rich bastards just want ta keep people out. Makes 'em feel like big shots I guess." Arlo wades downstream a couple of steps and pulls out a slender stick with the bark peeled off. The stick is strung through the gills of five, eight- and nine-inch horny-head chubs, one small twig left on the bottom to keep the fish from sliding back into the water. There is a piece of string tied to the top end, secured under a rock on the bank. "You want some of these here, Johnny. We gotta dress 'em."

"You know my Ma won't let me in the house with 'em. Just gonna be a bunch of bones anyway."

"Closer t' the bones the sweeter the meat." The mention of bones and meat restarts the giggles. When they can talk again Arlo pulls out his Barlow knife, "If I clean 'em, Mama'll cook em. They'll be a coupla bites—can't waste 'em." He scrapes each side of the little fish to take off the scales, makes a slit from their vents to their gills, pulls out the entrails, cuts off their heads, and tosses guts and heads in the water. "Watch for the crawdads."

They peer into the clear pool. A crawfish comes from under a rock and takes a long gut that has not washed downstream in its largest claw and starts backing toward its under-rock den. They smile, fascinated, at a brief tug-of-war that results when a larger crawfish attaches its pincer to the trailing end of the entrail. The smaller one manages to pull the prize away and make it to its hole. Arlo tries to splash the larger one onto the bank but it escapes under another rock.

"Wou'da made good bait. Them crawdad tails are the best."

Johnny rinses the worm bucket. Then Arlo throws the dressed fish in the pail and swishes his hands in the stream's cold water. They gather up their poles and Johnny starts up the hill.

"See ya, Arlo."

"Yep."

Arlo sets off in the other direction. Then he sees a piece of fish gut caught on a small twig. He stops to look at it. It's the size of the worms he was fishing with, caught six inches under the clear water, wriggling in the current like a live thing. Several small minnows are pecking away at it but they flush when the bigger crawfish materializes again, snatches the morsel and, making a small puff of sand, back-swims under a rock. Arlo laughs. He kind of wishes Johnny was here to see it, but he is kind of glad he isn't. He'll tell him about it. It was a pretty big crawfish.

Hemlock Hill is one of the small evergreen-covered hills that gain altitude like huge steps between the Elk River Valley and Hanging Rock Mountain. There are two ways to cross the hill: the road which follows a ridge between Grandfather Home Orphanage and the village of Banner Elk, and the shortcut trail which follows the foot of the bluffs parallel to the road, between the road and the river. The hill is dominated by tall hemlocks with a thick undergrowth of rhododendron and mountain laurel slicks. The short-cut trail is the quickest and most interesting way for Arlo to get home although it involves climbing over boulders and downed tree limbs and sliding down the bluff into the valley.

It is this route Arlo takes as he begins to weave his way through the bushes, pole in one hand and worm bucket with his catch in the other. He is going fast. He figures watching the crawfish will make him seriously late for supper, and his Mama will yell at him for sure. She has a loud voice and she will stand on the back porch and yell. It embarrasses Arlo, although there's usually not anyone close enough to hear her. She seems to worry a lot with his Dad gone and all.

Jack Lowe is sitting on a big hemlock log that lies along the edge of road that overlooks the shortcut. He has a pile of rocks in front of him, a couple the size of baseballs but mostly smaller. Jack is bigger than Arlo, and stronger. He is two years older, but just one year ahead in school because he started a year late. Jack has straight black hair cut real short so it stands up, dark eyes and a hard jaw. He is dressed in denim overalls and a short-sleeved shirt just like Arlo.

Jack sees Arlo walking up the shortcut trail long before Arlo sees him. The first rock he throws, a small one, rattles through tree limbs and lands about three feet in front of Arlo. Arlo doesn't know where it came from. He stops, looks around, and decides it was a pine-cone or an acorn, but he walks slowly forward, checking the trail ahead. The second hits a tree and doesn't make it to the trail but still makes enough noise to startle him. The third, a big one, grazes his shoulder just as he hears Jack laughing and sees him standing on the road.

"I see you, Jack. Quit it. You could'a hit me on the head."

"One of these 'uns will, ya little cunt," Jack shouts as he throws a handful of the small rocks that rain down on Arlo, who is as surprised at being called a cunt as he is by the pebbles. He doesn't know exactly what cunt means but he knows it's a cuss word and will probably send Jack to hell if Johnny's Ma is right.

Arlo begins to run, difficult on the rough trail. He has to slow down to climb over boulders and down trees. It's easy for Jack on the road to keep up, and he continues to throw rocks.

"Dammit, Jack. I ain't done nothin' to you. Jus' leave me alone. Why're you doin' this?"

"'Cause I don't like you, you little shit, that's why. You better run. If I catch you I'm a gonna whup your ass." Jack laughs. He throws a bigger rock that lands short.

The trail where Arlo is running begins to descend into the valley away from the road. If he can make it to the Exchange Grocery at the edge of Banner Elk before Jack catches him he'll be home free. Jack won't follow him into the village. There is only one more place where Jack will be able to throw rocks from the road and he will be able to pass it before Jack gets there. But it is there that his foot catches on a beech root, hidden under leaves, and he pitches onto the rocky trail, tearing his overalls, skinning his knee, and sending pole, bucket, and fish flying. The pole and bucket are easy enough to recover quickly. Four fish are also, and he puts them in the worm bucket. He looks for the last chub and finally spots it, just as Jack gets to the open spot above and resumes his rock throwing. Determined to get the last fish, which is the biggest, he crawls under a bush, grabs it, chucks it in the bucket, and is off again as two rocks hit him in the back.

"Fuck you, Jack. You can't beat me ta th' Exchange." He is running down hill now, fast, as he turns back and screams, "Bastard."

Fifty yards below the Exchange, gulping for breath, Arlo slows to a walk. His overalls are stained below a large rip from his bleeding knee and he is dusty all over. He doesn't know why Jack doesn't like him. He's never done anything to him. Well, at recess when Jack was punching him—he was always punching him—he hit Jack in the mouth with his lunch bucket and busted his lip. But Jack hit him back and bloodied his nose. They both had to go to see Mr. McCurry's and he whipped them with one of the willow canes he kept in the corner.

Anyhow, he's beat Jack to the Exchange and he's almost home. He can see his porch. Then he remembers his Mama and his lateness.

"ARLO." She is on the porch, as loud as she's ever been. "AAARLOOO." Even louder. "I see you down there. You get right on up here, boy. Oh, my goodness. You're gonna worry your poor Mama to death."

He thinks everybody in Banner Elk must hear her. He waves. Too out of breath to yell back. Close now to the porch.

"And just look at you. I'm gonna have to patch them overalls again. If I've patched 'em once I've done it a hundred. . .an' what on earth have you done to your knee? You ain't been in another fight have you?"

He holds up his bucket, "I got some fish."

She looks in the bucket. "Them things got dirt all over 'em. They ain't fit for nothin'."

"I can wash 'em."

"You come on in here 'n let me fix that knee." They go into the kitchen and she finds a bottle of Merthiolate. She washes his knee. The Merthiolate burns where his knee is scraped. Arlo can see his Mother has been crying. He doesn't know why she cries so much. He wishes she wouldn't do it.

"Wash your hands. I'll get supper ready. You can go get your sisters. When we're done you can wash your fish in the spring house."

After supper Arlo walks to the spring house at the lower edge of the pasture, followed by their two Guernsey milk cows. He washes the dirt, grit, and leaves off his fish and rinses his worm bucket and puts the little fish back in.

When he's done, he sits down on a big rock where he can see and hear the Elk River tumbling below. He takes out his knife and chips a piece off the cow's salt block and sucks on it. He picks a couple of wild strawberries that are in the pasture grass where he can reach them. Most of the strawberries are still green or blooming. He wishes he could fish for the trout he imagines in the big pool he can see. He thinks of the afternoon, of the talk with Johnny. For some reason a song starts going through his head. He doesn't know where he first heard it.

Cruising down the river, on a Sunday afternoon.

With one you love, the sun above. Waiting for the moon.

With one you love. Waiting for the moon.

With one you love.

Rosalee.

The Box of Lost Memories

Linda Juliano

Memories for Rachel Donovan are like seeds in the wind, never settling in one place long enough to grow roots.

Rachel hovers at the edge of the hallway and wrings her hands. The room is familiar in a way she can't quite grasp, but she knows it isn't her home. It doesn't smell right. Her house didn't smell like new carpet and flowers. At least she doesn't think that's how it smelled.

She moves to the dining table and lowers her aching body, fragile with age and illness, onto the hard wooden chair. Her heart leaps at the promise of...something. She reaches for the brown shoebox on top of the table and lifts the lid. The scent of old paper and tobacco wafts past her nostrils, leaving a tentative smile on her face.

"There you are," she says to the contents as the fragile pieces of her memory shift into place, and lost voices whisper in her ear.

Scooting to the edge of the chair, Rachel picks up a handful of photos and studies the faces. On some level deep in the recesses of her failing mind, she knows they're family and friends. Tiny butterflies flutter in her stomach when she comes to a black and white picture of a lean, handsome man standing beside her younger self. A name falls from her lips like a sweet kiss.

"Tom," she whispers, her voice cracking.

The love of her life and husband for more years than she can recall. Her heart aches with the love and the loss of him as the sweet scent of tobacco lingering in his pipe tickles the base of her nose. She wipes away the single tear on her cheek with the sleeve of her worn sweater. She doesn't remember when or how it happened, but she knows he's gone.

At the bottom of the box, she spies a small bundle of letters held together with a worn, pink ribbon. A spark ignites. A faint memory of sitting at a small, wooden desk, spilling her heart across the page.

"Tom," she whispers again.

With a deep, shuttering breath, she carefully unfolds a watercolor painting by a young child, maybe 4 or 5 years old. Her child? Yes. Elizabeth. A shadow of a memory of baking cookies with a curly-haired child drifts past, gone before she can form a complete picture in her mind.

As her memory begins to scatter, Rachel frantically pulls out Tom's pipe again, pressing it to her nose, drawing in the scent of tobacco—of comfort. In a jumbled, chaotic mess, the memories swirl in her head. A glimpse of Tom's blue eyes as they twinkle when he drops to one knee and holds out the prettiest diamond Rachel had ever seen. His large, callused hand tugging Rachel down the aisle after they say their vows. Tom lifting a dark-haired baby from her crib, tears glistening on his cheeks.

She squeezes her eyes closed, holding tight to the last memory as it floats away. Tom smiling around his pipe as he reaches for Rachel with one hand, pulling her onto his lap, the warmth of his body, his soft lips pressing against hers…

With the weight of fatigue, sadness, and confusion heavy on her shoulders, Rachel replaces the lid on the box and slumps back against the chair.

"Mother, are you all right?" comes an unfamiliar female voice at Rachel's side.

Rachel squints up at the stranger with the curly dark hair, then flinches when the woman strokes the thin skin of Rachel's arm.

A single tear rolls down Rachel's cheek as once again, the seeds of her memory scatter and disappear.

THE MASTHEAD

Hunter Bishop — Managing Editor/Founder

Peter Schaub — Associate Editor

Katherine Curran — Associate Editor

Made in the USA
Middletown, DE
05 September 2022

73255341R00040